Mer-boy

Contents

The Boat

Tara grew up by the sea, and had always loved the water.

"You are my water-baby," her mother would say.

"More like a smelly fish-baby!" teased Aisha.

Aisha was Tara's best friend. They were very different – Aisha was out-going, and Tara was the shy one – but it worked. They did everything together. Playing music, watching television, out on the bikes. They were like sisters.

Now, the two girls stood and looked at the boats.

"Come on, let's do it!" said Aisha.

Tara shook her hair out of her eyes and gave her friend a look.

"What?" said Aisha. "What's the problem?"

Aisha always looked like the nicest, sweetest girl in the world, with soft black curly hair and big eyes. But to Tara, Aisha's dark, sparkling eyes always gave the game away.

Her middle name was 'Trouble'.

Tara thought for a moment. They were both good swimmers. She was sure it would be safe.

"Okay," she said.

As the friends got into the boat, the wind began to blow. Tara felt a sudden chill.

A Sudden Splash

But she needn't have worried. It was such fun in the boat.

"Me first!" said Aisha (of course). She took the oars. It was easy. The boat slid along, fast and smooth.

"This is *so* cool!" Aisha said happily.

Tara put her fingers in the water. She smiled. She felt sleepy. She looked over the side and down into the darkness... Suddenly, Tara sat up.

"Look!" she shouted.

Aisha jumped. She dropped an oar, just as another gust of wind blew across the water and the boat rocked.

"Watch out!" shouted Aisha.

But it was too late. Tara was falling into the water…

The Song

Tara hit the water. As her head went under, everything went still. Then she heard a sound far away. Was it Aisha?

The boat bobbed above her. It would be easy to swim up to it. She kicked her legs.

But, just then, Tara felt something tug at her hand.

"Stay," sang a watery voice. It sounded like silver bells.

"Listen," sang the voice.

Tara frowned. What was the voice saying? It seemed important.

The song was all around Tara. She was happy to hang in the water, like a starfish, and listen.

And then a funny thing happened: Tara saw a face that she knew.

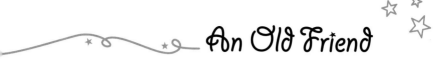

A pair of bright, sea-green eyes blinked open in front of her. It was a boy, about her age.

Her eyes opened wide, and she smiled. "It's you," she said.

Everything seemed to stop.

All her life, Tara had felt close to the sea. She had loved splashing in the surf when she was a little girl. One day she had seen the mer-boy under the water. Ever since then she had looked for him by the sea, and dreamed of him at night.

In her dreams he took her to his home, and showed her his sea-garden, and they played with the dolphins and baby seals. He was her special secret. But she had never seen him again. Until now.

Now the mer-boy was trying to tell her something.

"Come with me," he sang. He took her hand.

"Just for a while," she said to herself.

The boy tugged at her hand again.
But then Tara remembered Aisha.
"I have to go," she thought.
And she swam back up to the boat.

"Goodbye," sang the boy.

Mystery Message

The sun came out, and Tara dried off in the boat.

"How long was I under the water?" asked Tara. It felt like hours.

Aisha gave her a funny look. "About a second!" she said. "But you scared me. Try not to fall in again!"

"Listen. I have to tell you something," said Tara. And she began to tell her friend about the mer-boy. Aisha listened. She didn't speak for once.

"I know it sounds really odd," said Tara. "But it did happen. It really did! And he was trying to tell me something. Please believe me…"

She looked at her friend.
Aisha's dark eyes were smiling.

"Of course I believe you, silly," she said.
"But what I want to know is, *what* was
he trying to tell you?"

The friends talked it over for hours. But
they got no closer to finding the answer.

They walked home from the beach, arm
in arm, tired and happy.

Dream

That night, Tara had another dream.
In her dream, a boat rocked on a wild
and stormy sea. Tara heard the
mer-boy's voice singing. But this time
she could hear what his song said.
She could hear it loud and clear.

"Tell me again," said Aisha. The
friends were sitting in a café.

"Well," Tara said slowly. "In the dream
I'm under the sea, and there are rocks
all around me. There's this voice. It
says, 'Turn on the light.'"

"What do you think it means?" asked
Aisha.

"I don't know," said Tara. "But it has to mean something. I have the same dream every night."

"We'll just have to go down to the beach again tomorrow," said Aisha. "We'll find the mer-boy. I'll ask him myself!"

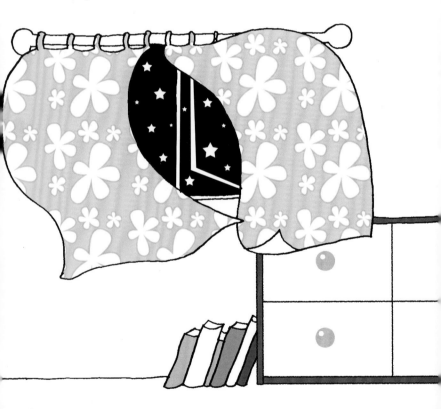

But Aisha never got to ask her question.
Because that night, as Tara went to
bed, a huge storm blew up.

The storm grew. The wind raged over
the sea and around the houses. It
howled all night, and threw the rain
down. Tara woke up. She knew what
the dream meant. She knew what she
had to do.

The Storm

First Tara ran to the window. She
needed to check. Then she ran to wake
her parents.

At first her mum thought Tara was
having a bad dream. Then her dad
thought it was a joke. "A very bad joke,
at 2 o'clock in the morning," he said,
crossly.

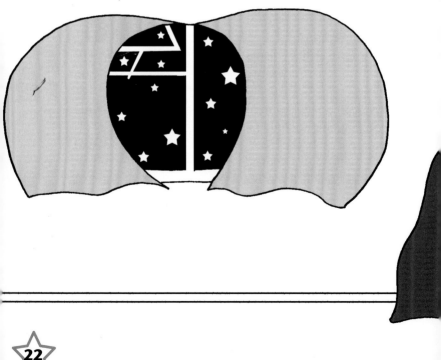

"Go back to bed," said her mother, more kindly.

Tara felt worried and helpless. She wanted to give up… but she thought of her friend, the mer-boy. She made up her mind. "I can't give up," she said to herself.

"Please, Dad! *Just look out of the window!*"

At last, Tara's dad got up.
He stared out at the night. He
scratched his head. "That's funny..." he
said to himself, sleepily.

Instead of the friendly beam of the
lighthouse, he saw only inky black sky.

"Dad, there's a boat," said Tara, all in
a rush. "There's no light. It will sail
onto the rocks. We have to turn on the
light!"

"Perhaps I'll just call the coastguard..."
her dad said slowly.

Tara felt herself relax. It would be
alright. But the land line was down.
And there was no mobile signal.
Dad began to look worried.

"Please, Dad!" she begged.

He nodded. "Just to be sure," he said.
Tara ran back to her bedroom and
threw on her clothes. It wasn't over yet.

Midnight Mission

The wind pelted them with rain, and shook the car. The waves crashed over the road. It felt like they were driving through a wall of water.

Slowly, they crept along the road. Every now and then, Tara could see the sharp point of the lighthouse, lit up by a flash of lightning. They drove on, through the heart of the storm.

Would they ever make it?

Suddenly the lighthouse was right in front of them.

Everything seemed to speed up. Tara's dad hammered on the door. He kicked it down, and found the still shape of the lighthouse man lying on the floor. Then it was phone calls, shouting, the flashing lights of the ambulance, and Tara heard talking, talking: to the doctors, the police, and the coastguards.

And at last, to Tara's relief, she saw the friendly beam of the lighthouse sweep across the sea. The beam lit up the rocks. A little boat was spinning in the stormy sea like a tiny teacup. But it was safe now.

Friends Forever

Once it was all over, Tara's little sea-side town went back to its sleepy ways. When Tara told Aisha about her adventure, she could hardly believe it herself. It seemed like another dream. But it *had* happened.

And Tara never really forgot.

A few years passed. Tara still loved the sea. She had grown out of games and bikes, but she still loved to walk along the beach, arm in arm with her good friend Aisha.

Now Tara was leaving home for a while. She went down to look at the sea. A light danced on the water. And then she saw him, standing in the waves.

Her heart jumped. She could almost touch him. The silvery song was all around her as it had been so many years ago. The mer-boy laughed. Tara looked into his sparkly eyes. She laughed too. She knew that he would always be with her. And she knew she would come back.

"Goodbye for now," she said.

He waved, and turned, diving into the surf with a joyful cry. She saw a flash of green tail.

And then he was gone.